CRUSHES COSTUME DAY

created by
JAY ALBEE

STONE ARCH BOOKS
a capstone imprint

Published by Stone Arch Books, an imprint of Capstone
1710 Roe Crest Drive, North Mankato, Minnesota 56003
capstonepub.com

Library of Congress Cataloging-in-Publication Data
Title: Riley Reynolds crushes costume day / written and illustrated by Jay
Albee. Description: North Mankato, Minnesota : Stone Arch Books, (2022)
| Series: Riley Reynolds | Audience: Ages 7-10. | Audience: Grades 2-3. |
Summary: Nonbinary fourth grader Riley and their friends are all in for
Dress Like Your Favorite Character Day, but when everyone at school asks
Riley for costume advice, they discover that the key to being a costume
visionary is active listening and a big imagination.
Identifiers: LCCN 2021970056 (print) | LCCN 2021058785 (ebook) | ISBN
9781666344042 (hardcover) | ISBN 9781666344080 (paperback) | ISBN
9781666344127 (pdf) Subjects: LCSH: Gender nonconformity—Juvenile
fiction. | Costume—Juvenile fiction. | Helping behavior—Juvenile fiction. |
Elementary schools—Juvenile fiction. | South Philadelphia (Philadelphia,
Pa.)—Juvenile fiction. | CYAC: Costume—Fiction. | Helpfulness—Fiction. | Gender
identity—Fiction. | Schools—Fiction. Classification: LCC PZ7.1.A4294 Ri 2022
(print) | LCC PZ7.1.A4294 (ebook) | DDC 813.6 (Fic)—dc23/eng/20211222
LC record available at https://lccn.loc.gov/2021970056
LC ebook record available at https://lccn.loc.gov/2021970112

Special thanks to Manu Shadow Velasco for their consultation.

Designed by Nathan Gassman

Printed and bound in the USA. 4882

TABLE OF CONTENTS

MX. AUDE TEACHES HELPFUL TERMS

Cisgender: Cisgender (or cis) people identify with the gender written on their birth certificate. They are usually boys or girls.

Gender identity: Regardless of the gender written on a person's birth certificate, they decide their gender identity. It might change over time. A person's interests, clothes, and behavior might be traditionally associated with their gender identity, or they might not.

Honorific: Young people use honorifics when they talk to or about adults, especially teachers. Mr. is the honorific for a man, Mrs. or Ms. for a woman, and Mx. is the gender-neutral honorific often used for nonbinary people. It is pronounced "mix." Nonbinary people may also use Mr., Mrs., or Ms. as well.

LGBTQ+: This stands for lesbian, gay, bisexual (also pansexual), transgender, queer. There are lots of ways people describe their gender and attraction. These are just a few of those ways. The + sign means that there are many, many more, and they are all included in the acronym LGBTQ+.

Nonbinary: Nonbinary people have a gender identity other than boy or girl. They may be neither, both, a combination, or sometimes one and sometimes the other.

Pronouns: Pronouns are how people refer to themselves and others (she/her, they/them, he/him, etc.). Pronouns often line up with gender identity (especially for cis people), but not always. It's best to ask a person what pronouns they like to use.

Queer: An umbrella term for people who identify as LGBTQ+.

Transgender: Transgender (or trans) people do not identify with the gender listed on their birth certificate. They might identify as the other binary gender, both genders, or another gender identity.

CHAPTER ONE

MONDAYS, AMIRIGHT?

"Riley! Where is your other shoe?" Dad called. He held one green canvas sneaker. He looked under the kitchen table for the other. His long hair flopped upside down.

"It's in the couch," Riley called back.

"*In* the couch?" Mama wondered aloud. She packed Riley's lunch into a lunch box and the lunch box into a backpack.

Dad pulled up the couch cushions. "Why are Mondays so hard? Ah! Got it!" he said, holding up both sneakers in all their glory. "Come put these on, Riley, or you'll be late for school."

"I can't find my lucky ribbon!" Riley said as they stomped into the living room.

Mama asked, "Why do you need luck today, Ry?"

"For *Monday*. Mondays are hard."

Mama laughed. "They don't always have to be. Here." Mama unclipped a barrette from her hair and clipped it into Riley's. Mama only let Riley wear her barrettes on special occasions.

"I think that'll help," said Riley.

"Here," said Dad, "you can have my scrunchie too."

"But then you'll get paint in your hair while you work. That's unlucky!" Mama took the other barrette out of her hair and clipped it into Dad's.

"Now everybody's lucky enough for a Monday," she said, laughing. "Now go to school!"

Mama waved as she headed down the sidewalk toward her subway stop. Riley jumped down the steps of their stoop.

A bunch of kids from Riley's block were waiting on the sidewalk with Mrs. Jackson from five doors down. Parents on Mifflin Street took turns walking the neighborhood kids to and from school. They called it the walking carpool.

"Hi, Riley!" said Mrs. Jackson. Mrs. Jackson was second grader Nelle's mom. "You are *rocking* that barrette-scrunchie combo!"

"Thanks!" said Riley.

"Now hurry up, people," said Mrs. Jackson. "We're running late!"

The kids trotted to keep up with Mrs. Jackson's long, quick stride. They were buzzing about Book Week and Dress Like Your Favorite Character Day on Friday. Riley loved dressing up. They loved coming up with costume ideas and making them just as much as they loved wearing them.

Georgie trotted beside Riley. "Riley, what will your costume be?" he asked. Georgie was a year older than Riley but only just as tall.

Riley had been thinking about their costume all weekend but hadn't picked one yet. They had been on a tutu kick lately, so maybe something with lots of poofy, floofy layers? Or maybe something to do with space? They had always wanted to make an astronaut suit out of cereal boxes. Could Riley and their parents eat that much cereal in a week?

"I'm not sure yet," said Riley. "So much to think about!"

"Whatever it is," said Georgie, "I'm sure it'll be great. You have great costume ideas. Like last Halloween? I don't know what it was, but I liked it!"

Riley beamed. They touched the barrette and then the scrunchie for luck. They hoped a just-right idea would come to them soon.

The walking carpool made it through the gate of South Philly Elementary just as the bell rang. The kids scattered to their classrooms.

Riley slipped into their seat just as Mr. Lane said, "A brand-new day and a brand-new week. Happy Monday, fourth grade! Let's get to it!"

CHAPTER TWO

A BRILLIANT COSTUME IDEA WILL COME . . . ANY SECOND NOW . . .

Later that day Riley's class had library time. Mx. Aude, the librarian, had set up a Book Week display in the school library. Books stood in rows behind yellow tape that read CAUTION/PRECAUCIÓN. Big, colorful signs said DANGER: AMAZING BOOKS and WATCH OUT, YOU MIGHT GET HOOKED!

Mx. Aude called Riley's class to the big blue rug. Mx. Aude changed the color of their cropped hair all the time. Today, it almost matched the rug.

"How're we all feeling about dress-up day on Friday?" Mx. Aude asked.

The class bubbled with excitement. Riley's best friend, Lea, bounced up and down. Riley's other best friend, Cricket, made the *beep-boop boop-boop* sound he made when he was being a robot computer. "Too exciting! Does not compute!"

"Okay, okay." Mx. Aude laughed. They held their hand high, which was their sign for quiet. "You're pumped. That's great." The class settled down.

"Now, everybody close your eyes. Think of a book that really gets you. Or a character you really understand. What do you think or feel about them? What would it be like to be them for a day?"

After a moment, Mx. Aude asked Riley's class to open their eyes again. Riley's mind was swimming with books and characters. Mx. Aude said, "Now, let's kick off Book Week with quiet time. What character did you just think of? Write a story about going on a new adventure with them."

Riley looked at the blank page. There had been so many characters in their mind when their eyes were closed. But now their eyes were open. A blank page is different from a blank mind. Riley watched Lea and Cricket writing their stories. Lea's feet went tippy-tap, like always. Cricket softly *beep-booped* to himself like Riley knew he would.

Instead of writing a story about a fictional character, Riley wrote about themself, Lea, and Cricket. Together they made astronaut suits and flew to the moon. They jumped around, leaving footprints in the dust. They met some aliens—green, round, cheerful—and set up a pizza shop. They lived happily ever after. Riley drew themself, Lea, and Cricket in moon suits and tutus, surrounded by happy green balls with antennae.

CHAPTER THREE

BIG QUESTIONS

At lunchtime, the playground buzzed with talk of dress-up day. Riley's classmate Olivia drew hearts on the blacktop with fat, colorful chalk.

She said, "I'm going to wear the flower-girl dress and tiara I wore at my cousin's wedding. I'll look just like a princess."

"Cool," said Riley. "Which princess?"

Olivia shrugged. "They're *all* my favorite." Then she sighed. "I guess I'll have to pick one."

"I'm dressing up as something scary," yelled Marco, bouncing a rubber ball.

Olivia rolled her eyes. "If anyone could like scary books, it'd be you, Marco."

Maddie pulled the end of her long braid. "I can never finish a scary book or movie. I hate being scared."

"I love it!" Marco yelled. Marco only had one volume on the playground. "When I'm president I'll make it so kids read only scary books." He kicked the ball across the playground and ran after it, yelling, "You'll see!"

Olivia yelled after him, "Not if I'm president first!"

Maddie watched Marco go. "I don't know what to do. I love reading, but I *hate* dressing up." Riley knew this was true. Maddie wore the same white-sheet-with-eye-holes ghost costume every Halloween.

"Do you think you could bring Chowder to school on Friday?" asked Riley.

"My dog? Sure, I guess," replied Maddie.

"Then she can be Walter from *Walter the Farting Dog.* Hang a cardboard sign around her neck that says 'Walter' and a sign on her butt that says 'Caution: Farts.'"

Maddie laughed. "That could work! I'll try anything if I don't have to dress up!" She ran after the rubber ball and Marco.

Tunde hung from the jungle gym. He sighed loudly, so everyone would hear.

"What's up, Tunde?" asked Riley.

"My favorite book is *Elmer and the Rainbow*," he said and sighed again, even louder this time.

"Why the sigh?" said Riley. "Elephants make great costumes, with the ears and the trunk and everything. And Elmer is so colorful!"

"I don't know how to make a patchwork elephant suit!" wailed Tunde. "Mom and Dad said I had to make my own costume this year because they're too busy."

"You could color in a white T-shirt," said Riley, "or go as the rainbow."

"If you go as the rainbow, I have an Elmer stuffie you can borrow," said Cricket.

Tunde's eyes went wide. "Really?" he asked. "That would be amazing! I can make a rainbow outfit no problem. Thanks, Riley! I never would have thought of that!"

Riley, Lea, and Cricket took some chalk and tried to invent a game of three-player tic-tac-toe. It didn't really work. But they had fun trying, and that's the important thing. Lea drew a spiral and asked, "What will you go as, Riley?"

Riley thought hard for a moment. Then they touched the barrette and scrunchie and, sure enough, had a just-right idea.

"I'm going to be a dragon. Maybe the one from *Prince and Knight*," they said.

Lea bounced up and down. *Prince and Knight* had been her favorite book since first grade. It was about a brave knight and a handsome prince who battle a dragon, fall in love, and get married.

"Group costume! Group costume!" she squealed. "Cricket can be the prince, and I'll be the knight! What do you think?"

"That's perfect, Lea," said Riley and Cricket at the same time.

"I don't think you can do that," said Olivia.

"Why not?" asked Lea.

"Because you're a girl. Can girls be knights? I've never seen one."

Lea looked worried for a moment.

"What about the *Princess in Black?*" asked Riley. Riley knew that both Lea and Olivia had read those books. So had most of the class.

"Ah," said Olivia. This was right in her princess-based area of expertise. "The Princess in Black is a *princess,* not a knight."

"But she's still tough like a knight, right?" asked Lea.

"True," said Olivia. "Actually, this gives me a great idea for dress-up day." And she trotted away without saying any more.

"You really think I can dress up as the knight from *Prince and Knight?*" Lea asked Riley.

Olivia had made her a little worried. "It's not too weird? I don't want to be laughed at," she said.

Sometimes getting laughs could be part of the fun of dressing up, but sometimes it was no fun at all. Riley's dad said that people laughed either because they got the joke or because they didn't know what to think. It was hard to tell the difference sometimes.

"If Tunde can dress up as a rainbow, and I can dress up as a dragon, you can *definitely* dress up as a knight."

Lea hugged Riley and Cricket. "You're the best! This is going to be great!"

The three friends spent the rest of lunch drawing knights, princes, and huge, glittering, magnificent, fire-breathing dragons in chalk all over the playground.

That night, Riley asked if Lea and Cricket could come over for the next few afternoons to work on costumes. Dad and Mama agreed right away. Dad said he would take them all to the secondhand store for materials.

The owner of the store was a funky lady named Marie. Marie never wore the same outfit twice. She knew everyone!

"And we can stop in to see Kwame in the craft supply shop," he said.

A few text messages and calls later, it was settled. Dad would take the whole walking carpool for costume supplies the next day.

CHAPTER FOUR

POOF, FLOOF, BEADS, AND MORE!

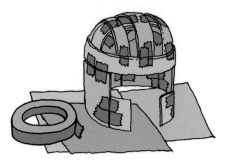

When they arrived at the store the next day, Marie pulled some boxes out from the back.

"You can have anything from these boxes you want," she said.

The kids dived into the boxes. They were full of great stuff—lengths of fabric and strange shirts and socks and hats and teapots and all kinds of things! It was everything Riley had hoped!

Cricket quickly found the perfect puffy-sleeved prince's tunic. It had a rip in it, but that would be easy to fix. Riley found what they were looking for too.

The other kids kept digging, hoping they'd know what they were looking for when they found it. Georgie picked some bead necklaces out of the box.

"Cool beads, Georgie. What are you thinking?" asked Riley.

Georgie sighed. "I want to dress up as Melissa from the book by Alex Gino. You know she's my favorite character." Riley did know that. Georgie talked about that book all the time. He and his mom read it together.

"But," Georgie went on, "dressing up as Melissa means wearing regular clothes. Where's the fun—the *theater*—in that?"

At the end of the book, Melissa acts on stage as Charlotte, in a play of *Charlotte's Web.*

"What if," wondered Riley, "you dressed up as Melissa-as-Charlotte? Then you'd dress up as your favorite character *and* your favorite thing!"

"Ew! I do *not* like spiders," said Georgie.

"No, no," Riley quickly replied, pulling out black spidery stuff from the boxes. "Not spiders. *Theater.* Like you said before: *theater.*"

Georgie gasped. "Wow! That's, like, *completely* perfect."

Third-grader twins Eva and Ellie were dressing up as characters from *Alice in Wonderland*. They were obsessed with that book.

Riley laughed. "You could go as Tweedledum and Tweedledee!"

Eva and Ellie did not look pleased.

"Maybe not," said Riley. "What about two bottles, one that says *eat me* and one that says *drink me?*"

Nelle and Georgie thought that was a great idea. Eva and Ellie did *not*.

"No!" said Eva. "We both want to be Alice. But I said it first. Ellie has to pick something else."

Ellie stamped her foot. "You did *not* say it first!"

"Did too!"

"What if—" Riley tried again.

"Wait!" Eva and Ellie said at the same time. "What if we're *both* Alice?"

Suddenly Eva and Ellie were on the hunt for blue dresses, white smocks, and hair ribbons.

"Well, that solves that," Riley said, watching them argue about whose Alice was going to be best.

CHAPTER FIVE

CRAFTING IS SERIOUS BUSINESS

"Riley?" Nelle asked. "Do you think you could help me find a costume too?" Second-grader Nelle was a shy kid who spoke in a soft voice.

"Of course!" said Riley. Nelle wanted to be *The Grouchy Ladybug,* because being grouchy is fun. In a box, Riley and Nelle found a skirt with red pom-poms on it.

"I could pull these off, stick them on pipe cleaners, and glue them to a headband for antennae!" said Nelle.

"Easy!" said Riley. They pulled out a good-sized scrap of sequined black fabric. "Do you have a red T-shirt?" asked Riley. Nelle nodded. "You could cut circles out of this and pin them on for that glamorous, spotty ladybug effect," Riley continued.

"It's not *too* glamorous, is it?" Nelle asked shyly.

"Not glamorous enough! Nelle, how do you feel about tutus?"

"Ooooooh," breathed Nelle. "I really like tutus."

"Then you can borrow my red one. It's super floofy," Riley said.

"Oh!" Nelle said, flushing as red as a ladybug. "Th-th-thank you."

When they were done, everyone walked next door to the craft supply store. The owner, Kwame, was a good friend of Riley's dad. He had plenty of shiny paper and pipe cleaners, googly eyes, and paints. He helped the kids find everything they needed.

"You all are going to look fantastic!" he said.

The carpool walked home with bags full of fabric, clothes, paper, and more.

At Riley's house, Dad pushed the kitchen table into the living room. He spread a drop cloth that used to be a sheet over the kitchen tiles.

Riley, Lea, and Cricket got started on their costumes right away. Dad stayed close to help with the hot glue gun. As they worked, they talked and laughed about what they were doing and thinking.

When Cricket needed some paper held in shape so he could glue it just right, Riley and Lea were there. When Lea was stumped about how to make the joints in her knight's armor, Cricket and Riley helped her. When Riley needed to know how big to make the dragon's snout, Lea and Cricket measured Riley's head.

They crafted right up to dinnertime. Mama picked up pizzas on her way home from work. Dairy-free vegetable for Cricket, gluten-free pepperoni for Lea, and peppers with extra pineapple for Riley. The only thing that stopped their happy talking were bites of steaming slices.

CHAPTER SIX

RILEY REYNOLDS, COSTUME VISIONARY

All Wednesday morning at school, Riley daydreamed about paper-mache dragon heads and before they knew it, it was lunchtime.

"Dress-up day is going to be so fun!" said Georgie.

"I know, right?" said Riley. "How's your costume-making going?"

"It's so much fun. And Mom is reading me *Melissa* again for inspiration," said Georgie. "Your idea is turning out so great, Riley. I told my whole class that you're a costume visionary!"

Riley grinned.

"In fact," continued Georgie, "some of them need help figuring out their costumes. Do you think you could come talk to them?"

"Oh!" said Riley. "Um." Georgie had called Riley a *costume visionary*. Riley liked the sound of it but wondered what it actually meant. Riley thought about helping Lea and Cricket with their costumes. And Tunde and Maddie, and Georgie and Nelle, too. Riley had made suggestions, but it worked best when Riley listened carefully and helped them come up with their own ideas. Maybe that's what being a costume visionary meant?

"Okay," Riley said, "let's give it a try."

The rest of lunch whizzed by as Riley talked to kids from Georgie's class. Riley asked lots of questions about favorite books, favorite characters, and what kind of supplies they had at home. Riley was very thorough.

After talking for a little while, and some suggestions from Riley and everyone else, the kid came up with their own idea. By the bell, everyone was buzzing with new costume plans. Riley was happy but exhausted. It was hard being a costume visionary!

After school on Wednesday and Thursday night, Riley, Lea, and Cricket worked hard on their *Prince and Knight* costumes. They met between Lea's soccer practice, Cricket's coding club, and Riley's drum lessons.

Lea worked on her knight. She covered pulled-apart cardboard cereal boxes in aluminum foil. She tried to get the shield extra shiny.

Cricket worked on his prince. He spent all of Wednesday evening cutting and gluing tiny aluminum foil stars onto a construction paper crown.

Riley worked on their dragon. They bent wire into frames. They tore and glued paper. They paper-mached a scary dragon head. They painted gnashing white teeth, bared roaring lips, and glaring yellow eyes. They cut red paper and orange cellophane for flaming dragon breath. They stuffed paper into a green stocking for a swishing dragon tail. They added egg cartons for dangerous dragon spikes. They cut shiny green paper for fearsome scales. They shaped sharp cones for dragon horns.

By Thursday night, the costumes were ready. Lea squealed with happiness. "The costumes look better than I even imagined!" she said.

"See you tomorrow," called Cricket as he and Lea headed to their homes.

Riley and Dad carefully moved the costumes into the living room and pushed the kitchen table back into place. Riley got out their homework. Dad got out the cookies and milk.

"You worked really hard these last few days, Ry. How's it feel?" Dad asked.

"Good." Riley dunked a snickerdoodle and bit into the yummy, soggy, milky cookie. "Really good. I'm so happy with how everything turned out."

"Nice. Tell me more," said Dad, reaching for his second cookie.

"It's like, I had this idea in my head about the dragon costume. It would have been amazing. Huge and flying from a crane and with speakers in it to make a terrifying sound. But that dragon wouldn't have worked, because we don't have any of that stuff."

"Oh no," said Dad, "did we lose my crane *again?*" Riley laughed.

"It was so cool hunting out supplies at Marie's and Kwame's. And then figuring out how to make a dragon out of what I had. And I like hanging out with Lea and Cricket."

"You three are a good team."

Riley beamed. "I can't wait for tomorrow!"

"Me, neither," said Dad, reaching for one more cookie.

CHAPTER SEVEN

AND THEN IT WAS FRIDAY

"Dad! Where is my other green sneaker?" Riley called. It was Friday morning. Riley had on the green leggings and sweater, socks of a dragon, and one green sneaker.

"On top of the fridge!" Dad called back. Mama sighed. She wasn't sure if the top of the fridge was better or worse than in the couch.

Cricket and Lea were sitting at the kitchen table, dressed in their costumes and ready to go. They had arrived at Riley's house extra early, bubbling with excitement.

Dad grabbed the shoe off the fridge with one hand and grabbed a slice of eggy bread with the other. He shoved the breakfast into his mouth and the shoe onto Riley's foot.

"Okay, team," he said. "Let's go!"

"Have a great day," Mama said, waving them out the door.

Riley's dad led Riley, Lea, and Cricket around the neighborhood, collecting walking carpool kids.

Lea's knight shone in the morning light and dazzled everyone's eyes. She was still figuring out how to walk stiff-legged.

"I bet this is how real knights walked," she said with a giggle.

Cricket's prince was so regal he looked more like a king. You could barely see the place where he'd patched up the tunic.

Georgie had added a hat to his Melissa-as-Charlotte costume. It was a black swim cap with a million googly eyes stuck on it. They swung and googled in all directions. It added just the right amount of dashing weirdness to Georgie's look.

"It's a bit tight," said Georgie, "but it really completes the outfit, doesn't it?" Riley had to agree. It was perfect.

Nelle floofed her tutu and twirled. The sun made the sequins in her spots glitter and gleam and sparkle. "Look, Riley," she said happily. She had new bright red sneakers on.

"Wow, Nelle, they're great!"

"Red is my new favorite color!" Nelle was the happiest Grouchy Ladybug *ever*.

Eva and Ellie were still arguing about whose costume was best. Everyone knew better than to take a side. They were both good Alices, in different ways.

The walk to school was a parade all the way down Mifflin Street.

At school, the teachers met the students at the gates. They formed two lines for the students to walk through. They clapped and cheered for every costume.

Mx. Aude was dressed as Medusa with a painted face and a pile of coiled plastic snakes on their head. Mr. Lane was a big bumblebee from his favorite picture book, *Bee*. They both looked fantastic.

A bunch of kids rushed over to Riley, who had never seen so many amazing costumes all at once.

"Riley!" said Tunde, with an Elmer stuffie tucked under one arm, "I'm a rainbow!"

He was a mix of colors, and even had two different-colored socks and two different-colored shoes. He had painted his face with the colors of rainbow. It looked best when he wiggled his nose.

"Fantastic!" said Riley.

Maddie was beaming at Chowder, the Farting Dog. Chowder was beaming from all the attention she was getting. "It's just right, Riley!" said Maddie. "I'm going to bring Chowder to every Halloween from now on!" Maddie squeezed a whoopee cushion to make a farting sound that made everyone laugh.

In a flashing tiara and long purple satin dress with a huge bow, Olivia really did look like a princess. Cricket bowed to her and said, "My lady." Olivia smiled wider than Riley had ever seen.

"Did you decide which princess you are?" asked Riley.

Olivia tied a black mask over her eyes and whispered, "I'm the Princess in Black." Riley and Olivia giggled.

Marco was dressed as Dracula. He kept laughing loudly in this spooky way. He held his eyes open really wide, which was odd and scary. Red makeup dripped from the corner of his mouth. Maddie refused to look at him.

Riley looked at their friends and could almost feel how happy they were in their costumes—Nelle was floofing her tutu, Lea beamed with happiness inside her tin-foil suit of armor, and Tunde was a spectacular rainbow.

Helping everyone find the perfect costume made Riley beam too.

Across the playground, Riley saw a group of Alice in Wonderlands. Riley didn't want to be around when Eva and Ellie saw them.

There was a fairy, a witch, and a brightly colored bird. A race car driver, a dinosaur, and a big, round strawberry. A firefighter, a pirate, and a long-horned unicorn. And here was a prince, a knight, and a dragon.

Riley Reynolds, Costume Visionary, felt light as a feather.

THE END

DISCUSSION QUESTIONS

1. If your school had Dress as Your Favorite Character Day, who would you choose? Why is that character or book meaningful to you?

2. Riley's classmate Maddie does not enjoy dressing up. What are some reasons someone might not enjoy dressing up? What are some reasons someone else might enjoy it?

3. Riley gets a lot of meaning out of helping others. In what ways did Riley help their friends?

WRITING PROMPTS

1. Write a story or article for the South Philly Elementary School newspaper about the dress-up day. You can interview Riley, Lea, Cricket, and others for your story.

2. When Olivia wonders whether girls can be knights, Lea is worried. Has anyone ever told you you couldn't do something because of your gender or gender identity?

3. Write a story or draw a picture of you and your favorite book character on a new adventure together.

MEET THE CREATORS

Jay Albee is the joint pen-name for an LGBTQ+ couple named Jen Breach and J. Anthony. Between them they've done lots of jobs: archaeologist, illustrator, ticket taker, and bagel baker, but now they write and draw all day long in their row house home in South Philadelphia, PA.

Jen's best costume ever was a railway conductor. J. once dressed up as the sun.

Jen Breach

J. Anthony